D0600677

The Boy Who Didn't Want To Be Sad

Published by
MAGINATION PRESS
An Educational Publishing Foundation Book
American Psychological Association
750 First Street, NE
Washington, DC 20002

For more information about our books, including a complete catalog, please write to us, call 1-800-374-2721, or visit our website at www.maginationpress.com.

Printed by Worzalla, Stevens Point, Wisconsin

Library of Congress Cataloging-in-Publication Data

Goldblatt, Rob, 1957-
The boy who didn't want to be sad / written and illustrated by Rob Goldblatt.
p. cm.
Summary: A boy gets rid of everything that might make him sad, but is sad anyway until he realizes that those things are also what make him happy and that one emotion is impossible without the other.
ISBN 1-59147-134-6 (alk. paper) -- ISBN 1-59147-135-4 (pbk. : alk. paper)
[1. Sadness--Fiction. 2. Happiness--Fiction. 3. Emotions--Fiction.]
I. Title.
PZ7.G56448Bo 2004
[Fic]--dc22
2003023546

ECO-FRIENDLY BOOKS
Made in the USA

10 9 8 7 6 5 4

The Boy Who Didn't Want To Be Sad

written and illustrated by
Rob Goldblatt, Psy.D.

Magination Press
Washington, DC

To all of us who took our ball and went home,
and to Carly, Emma, and Ethan,
who are brave enough to stay. — RG

Happiness: Lesson One

We push ourselves. Then we push our children. We want them to learn and to achieve. Why? So they will be happy. But how many of us teach our children how to be happy? Why don't we simply teach our kids that? Because not many of us know how.

Happiness seems elusive. It's not. Happiness isn't mysterious. It isn't expensive. It isn't something we achieve. It isn't about having more of this or being better than them. Happiness isn't even complicated. It is simple. It can be taught. This book is Lesson One, and the lesson is: Stay. Face emotions rather than flee from them. Even though it is scary, stay. Don't push feelings away, even the uncomfortable ones. Because it turns out that when we push away a feeling, we push away all feeling. How many of the problems that grownups try to fix with help from therapists, doctors, lawyers, personal trainers, 12-step programs, and so on are unhealthy behaviors that we develop to run away from our feelings? Let's teach our children (and ourselves) how to be happy. We can learn this early—the earlier the better. So we begin…

Lesson One. Stay.

There once was a boy who didn't want to be sad.

So he made a decision and he made a plan. He would get rid of everything that made him sad.

The boy wanted to get away.
As all people do
sometime in their lives.
Lying in his secret place
in the shade,
he felt as if he could
see the whole world
laid out before him.
The trees swayed
above. The leaves
rustled softly.

**And he
was happy.**

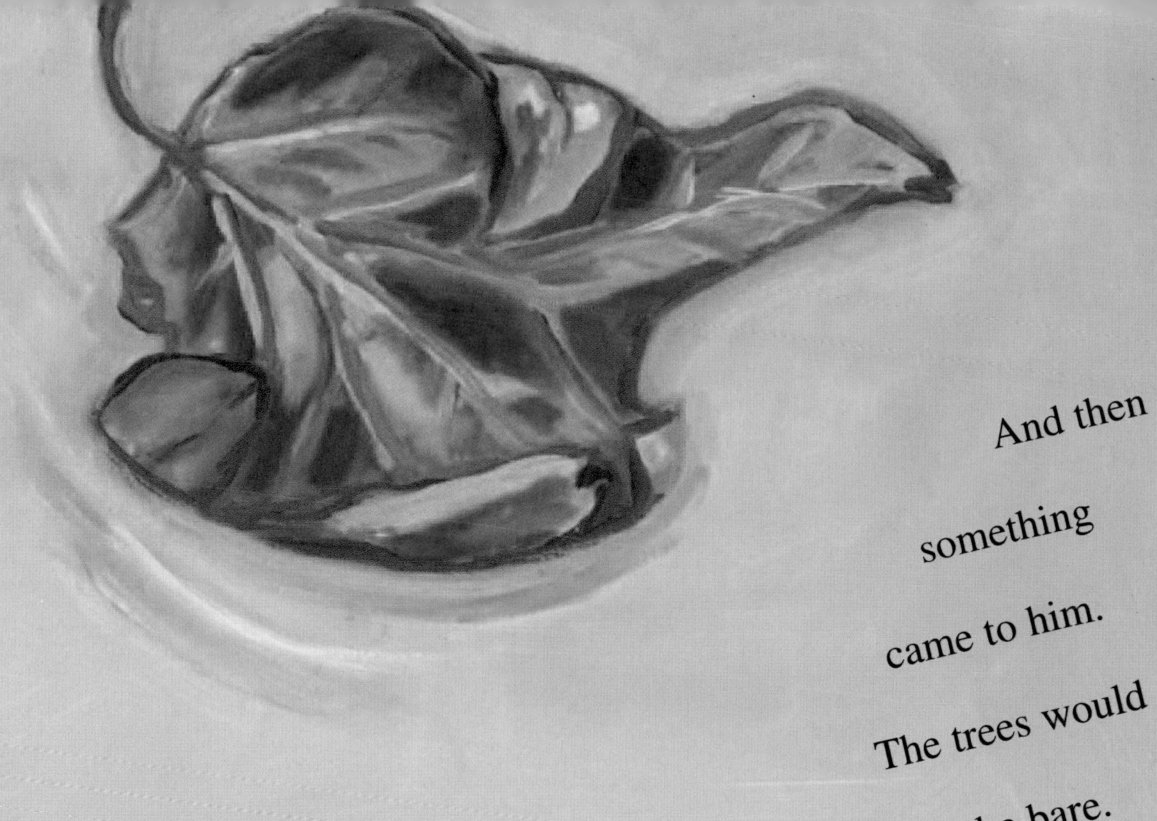

And then

something

came to him.

The trees would

soon be bare.

That made

him sad.

He had to get as far away from the beautiful old tree as he could. He stayed inside after that with his golden retriever named Goldie, his gerbil named Goldie, and his goldfish named Goldie. He watched video after video and flipped through a thousand channels.

But every story had sad parts.

So he stayed in

his room after that.

Bored.

He began stacking

his old blocks.

Before he knew it,
he had built a tower
to the ceiling.
He had done
something he was
proud of. As all
people do at times
in their lives.
His whole family
came to see.
His little sister
was so excited,
she jumped.
She jumped and
jumped and...

uh-oh!

So, what's
the point of doing
anything anyway?
Blocks fall, toys break,
game pieces get lost.
He'd had it with
everything.

He quietly picked up all his things,

walked to the window, and

...threw them out!

He felt a twinge inside
as they fell. Still, he always
had his family. His parents knew
how to make him happy with two words:

MINT CHIP!

And he was deliciously happy until...

his sister whined,

"I want some!"

"No," he declared.

"Share your ice cream,"

said his father.

"No!"

His mother gave her deadly warning,

"I'm counting to three."

She counted

to three.

And on three,

the boy threw

his family out!

And he was

happy.

Then the

phone rang.

His friends!

Hooray!

But then, what if

they stopped calling?

He would be sad again!

NOOOOOOO!

So the boy was alone, all alone, except for Goldie, Goldie, and Goldie. And he was happy. They would never make him sad. Never! Not as long as they lived. As long as they lived? Uh-oh.

So the boy locked the doors.

He shut the windows.

And he pulled the drapes.

He sat by himself in an empty room.

Finally, he was completely safe.

Nothing could make him sad now.

Then, he looked up. Oh no, the light bulb!

When that burned out he would be miserable!

He had to get rid of it. He hesitated. It was all he had left.

But before it could burn out, the boy unscrewed the bulb.

And he was...

SAD!

But how could that be?
He had gotten rid of everything
that could possibly make him sad.
Things looked completely black.
As they do to all people
sometime in their lives.
Then he realized something
amazing, something
totally crazy.

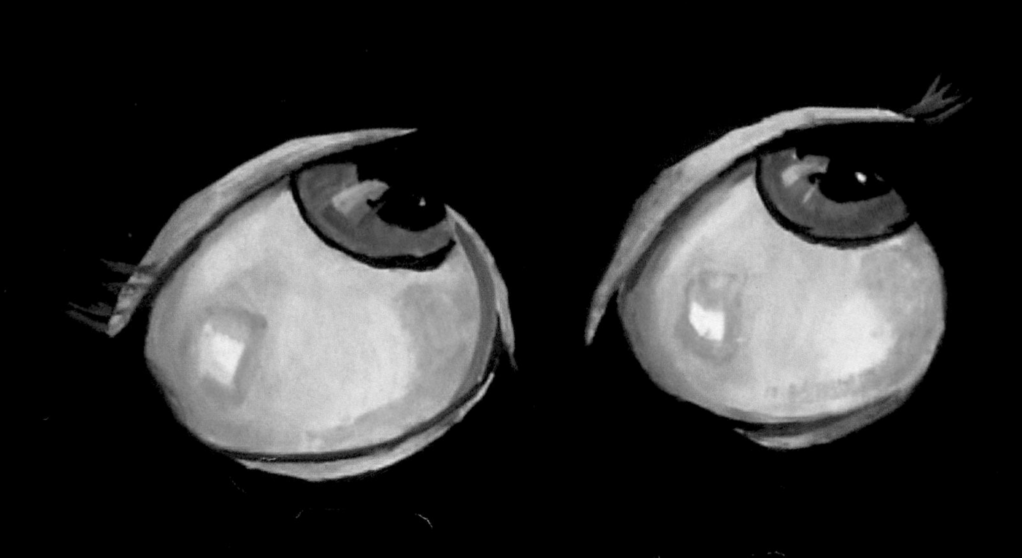

The things that made him sad

were also the things that

made him HAPPY.

In fact, the sadder he was to lose something,

the happier he must be to have it.

Wow! He was doing it all backward!

So the boy made a decision

and he made a plan.

He went back
out into the
world and
took back.
EVERYTHING!

And he lived happily ever after. And sadly. And laughing hysterically a whole lot. And feeling guilty a few times. Downright miserable now and again. Embarrassed. Intensely shy sometimes. Constantly curious. Full of wonder always. And totally loving life. Ever, ever after.